LITTLE MONSTER'S NEIGHBORHOOD

by Mercer Mayer

to Joel

MERRIGOLD PRESS • NEW YORK

This is my neighborhood.

I live in the tan house with the blue roof at the edge of town.

My best friend lives around the corner.
We play ball together and have tricycle races.

We have a secret clubhouse in an old tool shed,
and we have a secret password that nobody else knows.

We like to go shopping with my mom.
First we stop at the Grithix Gas Station.

NO
LEAD

GRITHIX
GAS
is
GOOD
GOOD
GOOD

Mr. Grithix lets us look at an engine.

We shop at Mrs. Gorpley's Market.
She has almost everything.

Sometimes, on our way home, we pass Mr. Bombanat, the policemonster.

On Sunday, I go to church with my family.

After church, we
have ice cream sodas
at the drugstore.

We do special things on Sunday afternoons. Sometimes we visit Mr. Yalapappus's farm. He lets us help feed the animals.

One Sunday, there was a firemonster's parade. I got to ride through town in a fire engine.

In summer, we go swimming in the park.
My sister can swim already, but I'm still learning.
My best friend says he would rather fish.

In winter, we go ice skating in the park.
I fall down a lot.

In my neighborhood, someone is always coming to our house.

The milk monster brings the milk first thing in the morning.

Then comes the papermonster with the morning paper.

The Mail Trollusk delivers our mail just before lunch. Sometimes I even get a letter.

The garbagemonsters pick up the garbage. Their truck grinds it up with a roar.

When something is broken, a repairmonster comes. Today the plumber came.

This afternoon, my mother told a monster that she didn't need a new vacuum cleaner.

When my mom and pop go out
for the evening, a baby-sitter comes,
but I'm no baby.

When I need a check-up,
I go to Doctor Windbag's office.
It's right in his house.

Sometimes my sister takes me to the library. We can choose a book to take home for a week. I show the librarian my library card and he stamps my book.

We run home past the old haunted house
but we're not really scared.

At night, before I go to bed, I have milk
and homemade cookies. My mom makes the
best cookies in my neighborhood.